When I Left My Village

❖ ❖ ❖

When I

❖ Maxine Rose Schur ❖

Left My Village

Pictures by Brian Pinkney

New York ❖ Dial Books for Young Readers

J S

HISTORICAL FICTION

Published by Dial Books for Young Readers
A Division of Penguin Books USA Inc.
375 Hudson Street
New York, New York 10014

Text copyright © 1996 by Maxine Rose Schur
Pictures copyright © 1996 by Brian Pinkney
All rights reserved
Designed by Nancy R. Leo
Printed in the U.S.A.
First Edition
1 3 5 7 9 10 8 6 4 2

Library of Congress Cataloging in Publication Data
Schur, Maxine Rose.
When I left my village / by Maxine Rose Schur ;
pictures by Brian Pinkney. — 1st ed.
p.   cm.
Sequel to: Day of delight.
Summary: An Ethiopian Jewish family leaves their oppressed
mountain village to make a difficult and treacherous journey
in the hope of reaching freedom in Israel.
ISBN 0-8037-1561-7. — ISBN 0-8037-1562-5 (lib. bdg.)
[1. Jews — Ethiopia — Fiction.]   I. Pinkney, J. Brian, ill.   II. Title.
PZ7.S3964Wh 1996   [Fic] — dc20   94-45799   CIP   AC

*The artwork was prepared using scratchboard, a technique
that requires a white board covered with black ink. The ink is
then scraped off with a sharp tool to reveal the white.*

❖ ❖ ❖

For Stephen
— M.R.S.

For Andrea
— B.P.

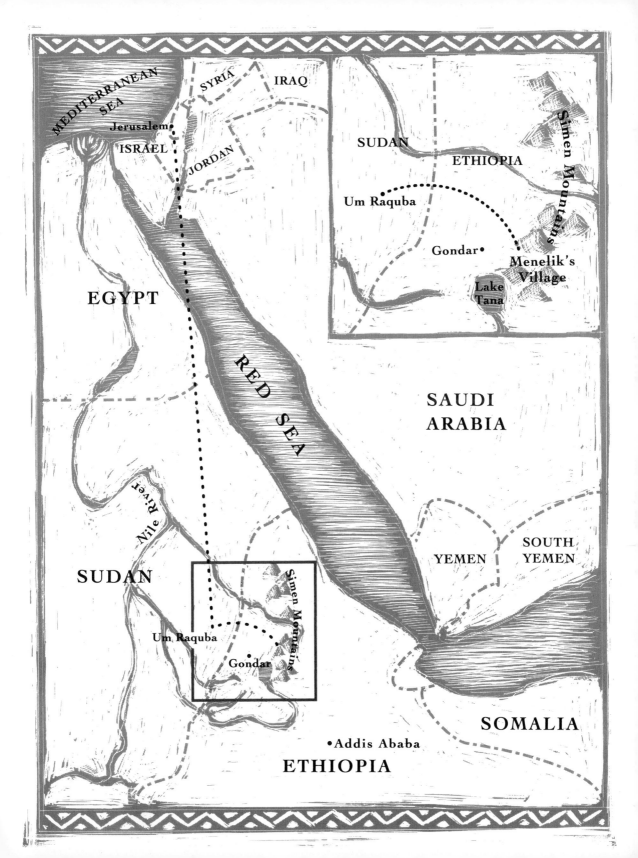

"Deliver me and put me with Thy people Israel,
for Thou art just, O Lord."

H

IGH IN THE MOUNTAINS where the clouds can be touched lies a poor and hungry land. This is the Gondar province of Ethiopia. And here, up a path twisted as a snake's track, sat my village.

My village had few trees and little rain, so that under our bare feet the earth felt hard and dry. With its round mud huts my village seemed like any other in Ethiopia. But if you looked closely, you'd have noticed one hut that was different. On its thatched roof rose an iron Star of David. This hut was our *mequrab* — our synagogue, for we are the *Beta Israel*, the Jews of Ethiopia.

9

Beta Israel, that's what we call ourselves, although other Ethiopians call us *Falashas* — strangers.

"Why do they call us strangers?" I once asked my mother. She was bathing my little brother, Simcha, in one of the big pottery bowls she had made.

As she plucked him out to dry him, she answered, "Because, Menelik, they do not understand our ways and so are afraid of us."

I knew that many Ethiopians feared us, for I had seen their fear at the marketplace in Gondar. My father, like almost all Beta Israel men, was a blacksmith. Every few months he, my mother, and I would walk the long way down the mountain path to the town of Gondar. Our journey would take most of the day, but when we got to the marketplace, my father could sell the tools he'd made, and my mother, her bowls and jugs. If we were lucky we'd be paid fifteen *birr*, enough to return home with flour, oil, salt, sugar, and sometimes a chicken or two.

Our customers were Muslim and Christian Ethiopians. They looked and spoke the same as we did. Because we bathed so much in the river, they called us "the people who smell like water." Yet often when we'd walk through the ragged crowds, we would hear the cry "Falasha Buda!" and know that we were being called people of the Evil Eye. The ignorant among them believed that because we worked with metal, we were sorcerers. They believed we could poison water by looking at it, or make someone sick with our glance. They believed that at night we turned into bloodthirsty demons — with bodies of foxes and snouts of pigs.

And so we Beta Israel lived apart from our neighbors. Because we were not allowed to own land, we became sharecroppers, tilling the soil for the rich landowners, living in scattered villages so isolated from others, many people did not even know we were there.

Our tools were forged in the fire, and our days shaped by the sun. Before it rose, we were already at work, making sickles, axes, and knives. The blows of our huge hammers rang through the village and echoed in the valleys. When the sun slid below the mountains, we'd come home tired, soot-stained, and sweaty.

A few men in our village were not blacksmiths. Some wove *shammas*, long white robes, to sell in Gondar. Some fished in Lake Tana, while others planted and harvested *teff,* the grain from which we made *injara,* our round, flat bread.

The women worked hard too: building fires, cooking stews, driving cattle, carrying babies, and grinding teff. The boys helped their fathers, and the girls, their mothers. From the time when woodcocks first crow to the darkening time when swallows fly, everyone worked.

One day a man too big for his donkey, and with a sugar bag strapped to his back, rode up the path. He said he was sent from the government in the capital, Addis Ababa, to teach us. And so every morning the children did not work, but listened to this man. He taught us letters in our language, Amharic. He taught us how we could string these letters together like beads on a necklace to make words. He taught us numbers big enough to count the stars over our village. And he unrolled a great piece of paper. "All Africa," he said, showing us on this map how Ethiopia sat near the top, horn-shaped and blue.

But our teacher did not stay long. "Too much work! Too little food! No electricity! Too poor!" So before winter, down our path he rode. Pencils, paper, and all Africa — back in his sugar bag.

When he left, my mind hungered for more words, for bigger numbers, and to know of our continent cracked into colored shapes. But after a while, as the long days again filled with work, school became only a memory.

Our life was hard, yet *Sanbat,* our Sabbath, brought us joy. Before sundown on Friday all work in our village stopped. We put away our tools and bathed in the cool green river. Then we would dress in clean shammas to welcome the Sabbath. That evening and all the next day we did no work. It was a day for eating together, resting, and most of all, for praying. We prayed for a good crop and for peace in our village. We prayed that enough rain would fall. And we prayed that one day we would see Israel. It was as distant as Paradise, but Israel was our ancestral land, our dream, and we longed to go there.

This is the way we lived. From new moon to new moon. Year after year. Century after century. We lived this way until the year I turned twelve—when the bad things happened.

The bad things began early one night when Solomon, the young weaver, ran through our village. "Arras Ambiba is in flames!" he shouted. "Higher than the flames of

affliction! Arras Ambiba is burning to the ground!" We ran out of our huts to the sound of his wild cries.

16 "Pity on us, oh God-King!" Solomon wailed.

My father gripped Solomon's arms, holding them fast, for they shook like branches in the wind. "Tell us with your mind what your heart is crying," Father commanded.

Like a drowning man, Solomon drew in his breath and then his words came out in a torrent.

"I went to Gondar yesterday to sell my shammas, and as I walked back tonight, I saw a bright light in the far distance. The light grew larger; it glowed like the sun. As I watched it, a car drove up. The men inside were drunk from *tala*. They were hooligans hired by the landowners, and they pointed a pistol at me and shouted, 'Where are you going, hyena-boy?' When I did not reply, one of them yelled, 'We have just burned a Falasha village, and we will burn others if you Falashas try to steal land. You will work it like the dogs you are. You'll never own it!' Then he shot at me but his aim was poor. Unhurt, I slumped to the ground. Thinking they had killed me, they drove off laughing."

That night the elders of our village met in the mequrab to discuss what Solomon told us. The next morning my father explained to my mother and me what the elders had said.

He told us that the government had passed new laws saying all Ethiopians should own land, not just the rich, the poor too — even the Beta Israel.

"But the rich landowners refuse to give up any of their land," said Father. "They hire their own armies to travel the countryside and threaten the sharecroppers. 'Do not even try to buy land!' they warn, and they make their words stick with terror — kidnapping, torturing, murdering."

"We should go to the capital," Mother said. "The government in Addis Ababa must know that the landowners are doing these terrible things to the people, and stop them!"

"We cannot," Father answered with anger in his throat. "If the landowners found out we went to the government, they'd shoot us all!"

"Then what can we do?" Mother asked sorrowfully, pulling her shamma tight over her head as she always did when she was worried.

"We will stay calm," Father said. "That is what the elders advise. We will wait and see what happens."

From that day on, life in our village changed. Every day we heard of another Beta Israel village burned by the landlords. We heard of our people being sold as slaves, beaten and murdered. Some young men left. They tried to walk across Ethiopia all the way to Kenya, but they were caught and never seen again.

Rather than help us, the military government began to threaten us too. They hated Israel and thought us traitors for wanting to go there. From Gondar, army jeeps rumbled up our path. The government soldiers warned us, "Do not even try to leave Ethiopia or you will know the *bastinado*." The bastinado! To be hung upside down and beaten on the soles of your feet!

Now we were afraid of the landowners *and* the government soldiers. We became suspicious of everyone. We dug a hole deep into the ground and hid our money. No longer did we go to the Gondar market, for it was dangerous to be on the road. Father sold the sickles he had made to a Christian friend in a neighboring village, and for a while we traded tools for food.

Then the drought came. In the flat land no rain fell.

The rivers turned to slime, the trees withered, and the wildflowers did not come. All across Ethiopia people died.

Suddenly everyone wanted to leave. When news came of camps in Sudan where Ethiopians could get food, thousands fled there.

In our mountain village it rained a little, but not enough. The teff crop that year was small. We ate injara made from the teff flour we had left, and we boiled wild grass. What will we eat when this is gone? I wondered.

In the early evenings I no longer played ragball with my best friend, Josef, and the other boys. Instead I helped my mother search for wild blackberries, and I gathered the soft grass that grew near the creek's edge. At dusk one day I was picking this grass and piling it into a basket when I heard a sound of breathing. I turned to see my father standing behind me. His strong face was still as stone. I knew that he had been watching me. And I sensed that he had something important to say.

"Menelik," he said, his voice supple and steady as river flow, "we must go away."

"Go?" I repeated in surprise.

"We must leave our village and go away forever."

I was so shocked, I said nothing.

"Our journey will be a long one," Father continued.

"How long?" I asked.

"Past where the hyenas howl," he answered. "Past the high mountains, past the long rivers of Ethiopia."

"Are we going to Sudan?" I asked. "The country where people have skin even blacker than ours?"

"Yes, and from there to Israel."

Israel! When my father said the word, my heart beat like a Sabbath drum.

"We are going to Israel, the land of the Jews. The place where we can be free." Father stepped toward me and placed his big hands, like a mantle, on my shoulders. "Mother is worried, for the government forbids us to go to Israel. We will be brave, but as it is forbidden, we will not speak of it. Do you understand?"

I nodded.

Father looked into my eyes. "Tell no one," he warned again. "No one."

❖ ❖ ❖

The next day we packed our things. Mother made travel bread, and we wrapped the flat *quitta* in a large cotton cloth. We also packed dried chickpeas and dried beef. I dug the money up from the hole, and Father carried it in a pouch under his shamma. He also packed some of his tools into a goatskin bag. Mother folded two blankets into a pack to carry on her back.

When we had finished, I looked at the mud walls of our home where clay pots, baskets, and weavings still hung on nails. Reading my mind, Mother said, "It's all right, Menelik, the neighbors can use them."

When night fell, I went to the dried dung heap and stuffed some into a small burlap sack, for Father had said we might need it along the way for fuel.

"Menelik . . . Menelik!"

Startled, I looked up to see in the moonlight the silhouette of my friend Josef. He approached me whispering, "I came to say good-bye to you."

"What do you mean?" I asked. "I am not going anywhere."

He said nothing. Tension hovered like a swarm of mosquitoes in the air between us. "Here, this is for you," Josef said at last, pressing into my hand a slingshot. It was as long as my foot, made of acacia wood, and polished smooth. "You're the one in our village with the best aim," he said. "I made the slingshot especially for you. You might

need it . . . " I knew he wanted to add, "where you are going," but he didn't.

"Thank you," I whispered, then I wanted to say something else too. That I would miss our ragball games. That I would miss him. But I couldn't, so I just listened to his footsteps as he stole away.

Very late at night, we left. Father slung his bag of tools over his shoulder and took Simcha by the hand. Mother carried the blankets, and I, the food and a water tin. For hours we walked along the road that led north into the Simen mountains. Before dawn Father said, "The main roads are dangerous by day. People would see us and know we are leaving. Now we must leave the road and enter the forest. But remember the forest is not just a refuge for us, but for the *shifta*, the gangs of bandits and murderers who hide there."

We walked for what seemed a very long time, climbing higher and higher into the mountains. We went quickly and in single file, for the paths were narrow and rimmed the edge of steep canyons. We were still walking when we heard the sunrise songs of birds. "I'm hungry!" Simcha suddenly cried out. So at last, very tired and hungry ourselves, we stopped. We sat at the edge of a mountain crest, and as the sun rose, ate our breakfast.

Far below us we could see valleys spotted with baobab and mimosa trees, and laced with narrow green rivers. A falcon floated lazily on a current of air.

"Are we almost in Israel?" Simcha asked, licking his lips to trap every crumb of travel bread.

"Shaaa," Mother murmured, hugging him, "we've only begun."

"How long will it take us to get to Israel?" I asked.

"Two weeks, even if we go quickly," Father answered. "For we are not going the stealthy and straight way of the leopard, but the wary, winding way of the ibex. And we can travel only at night. During the day we will hide ourselves and sleep."

"What will we eat?" Simcha asked, for his mind was always on his stomach.

Mother smiled. "We will feed you travel bread and juniper berries, Little Lamb. And we will boil our dried meat — nice and tasty."

"And we will feed you river fish to swim in your belly," Father teased.

"And I will shoot a big duck for you," I said. "See, I will do it with my slingshot, just for you."

Simcha reached out happily to hold my slingshot, and as he did, Father said gravely, "We have not enough food to last us two weeks, so we must find it as we go, in the trees, the rivers, and on the plains."

It was when Father told us this that Mother pulled her shamma tight over her head and sighed, "All over Ethiopia people are escaping together."

"Yes," Father said, "they are escaping the famine, but we are escaping persecution. That is why we are in more danger."

"I know," Mother persisted, "but I have heard even Beta Israel families are escaping in groups. Only we are traveling alone."

"We are safer alone," Father said firmly. "What is more easy to spot — a crowd of people — or four?"

"But sometimes," Mother replied just as firmly, "there is protection among others."

"We are among each other," said Father, "and that is enough."

Every day we followed Father's plan, walking at night

and resting in the day. Whenever we stopped, Father carved an arrow into a tree so that if we got lost, we could go back and see from which direction we came. And each day in the mountain forest we filled our tin with creek water and found food: tiny silver fish we caught in the creeks; wild figs, nuts, and berries; and pigeons that I killed with my slingshot. Skirting far around the cliffside villages, we saw no one in the first week. But one morning, as we were preparing to sleep, we heard voices close by and then the sound of guns. *"Shifta!"* Mother whispered, her eyes wide with terror.

"Ho, look at these scarecrows!"

Three men dirty as Gondar beggars stood before us. The men were young and their faces cruel. As if we were prey, they aimed their rifles at us. I stood between my mother and father, and it seemed I heard their heartbeats stronger than my own.

"What have you scarecrows got in there?" one of them asked, eyeing Father's toolbag.

"Nothing but ironmonger's tools," Father replied, "of little value."

The man inspected the bag, then sneered, "You must

be Falasha, for only Falasha do this dirty, black magic work."

The man took Father's bag and flung it hard against a tree so that the tools flew out and scattered on the ground. My father was twice as strong as he and the other two put together, but they had guns, so he could not fight them.

One of the men had pointy teeth like a dog's. Now he walked over to our packs, pushing my mother aside so that she fell. The other men laughed at this, and then all three began rifling through our packs. "Quitta!" they shouted greedily when they saw our travel bread. They grabbed it along with our dried meat, our great supply of figs, and our chickpeas too. It was all the food we had, and they took it.

Simcha began to cry, and his short anguished wails were like sharp knives that slashed the air again and again. "Shut up!" the pointy-toothed man warned Simcha, yanking his arm roughly.

My mother cried out, and my father, who had been silent all the while, now stepped up to this man and said, "Do not touch him."

I thought surely they will shoot us all dead, but the man, startled by the rage in Father's voice, stepped back. Just then there was a crashing sound in the trees followed by an unholy scream, and the men, like ghosts that must disappear before dawn, grabbed their plunder and fled.

We were so amazed to still be alive that for a long time after they left, none of us said a word, but sat on the ground like mourners as Simcha continued to wail. Through the trees we saw a giant gelada baboon run, and knew that this animal had made the terrifying noise. Holding Simcha close, Mother rocked back and forth to comfort him, murmuring fervently, *"Yatabarak Egziaber Amlak Israel!"* Blessed be the Owner of the World, the God-King of Israel!

Eventually Mother, Simcha, and I slept while Father kept watch over us. When darkness fell, we continued our journey—now without food. Father carved fishhooks out of eucalyptus twigs, but as we came down from the mountains westward into the plains, we saw that the rivers had dried up months ago. There were no fish to be caught and no animals to be shot. There was almost no vegetation. As far as we could see, there was only dry land and rocks. The few acacia trees were thin as skeletons, but we hungrily ate their skimpy leaves. Without food and with our water supply low, we walked slowly. Slower and slower each day.

On this flat land the sun was hot, and the shade was small. In the day when we stopped to rest, the sun beat down on us so hard, I feared we'd all disappear, just as scraps of iron melt in a flame. In the night we were no more comfortable, for a great gale blew across the black desert like wind from some infernal bellows. The strong wind seemed to fan even the stars, making them burn brighter than normal — like glowing coals.

We had been traveling so slowly that one morning Father said it would take us another five days to reach the border of Sudan. We had walked nearly the whole night, and at these words Mother burst out madly, "We haven't food and water for one day, let alone five! Look at your child!" Mother screamed, picking up Simcha and holding him out in front of her as if he were a sacrifice. "Look at your child! I will find a village and sell my bracelet for milk!"

"There are no villages around," Father replied, trying to keep his voice steady, "and even if there were, we must

not risk it!" Then my mother, who had been strong as ancient Sarah, hugged Simcha to her and wept bitterly. Father wrapped his arms like a shamma around them both. He spoke words of comfort to us. "We must not give up now," he said, "or take foolish risks. We will give Simcha all we have and keep going. We will rest well and then continue on, and if we have faith, in five days we will be at the border of Sudan. We are tired now, that is all."

My father was tall, strong, and brave, yet his words gave me little comfort. For now he seemed to me a great tree without roots, and I feared for us.

I was so afraid, I dared not say anything. I remained silent and saw how Mother's eyes flowed with tears. I saw how her copper bracelet could no longer stay on her wrist. I saw how Simcha no longer talked, and how his skin had become like the skin of an old man and the whites of his eyes yellow. Our spirits were low, our bodies aching, and our stomachs empty.

Father made each of us beds from the fallen acacia branches so we would be protected from the poisonous

snakes that lived in the dry soil. My parents and Simcha fell asleep quickly, but I could not sleep. I took our empty tin and slipped away. Maybe I will find cactus fruit for Simcha to eat, I thought as I walked, not knowing where. It seemed I had walked a long way when I came to a shallow ravine. I climbed down, not thinking of anything but food. Then I heard it . . . a sound soft as a kitten's purr. The water sound! I imagined the water cooling my parched lips. I followed the sound and came to a stream trickling down from the hills and hidden all around by thornbush. I was about to fill the tin when I saw a partridge on the opposite bank. It sat on a low branch, still as an owl.

I thought of this fat bird, roasted and juicy, but I had not brought my slingshot with me, and if I went back to get it, the bird might be gone. I picked up a round stone, a little bit smaller than my hand, then I aimed carefully. Zing! With one swift pitch I killed the partridge, and it dropped to the ground with a plump thud. I went to pick up the bird, but as I returned to the other side, I saw out of the corner of my eye something upstream that made my heart freeze.

A lion had come to drink. He was so close to me that I could see his long tongue lap the water. I had never seen a lion before, and now his great body and huge head filled me with terror. "Lord, King of Israel, protect me!" I prayed silently. I dropped the partridge and stood still as a rock. The lion looked up in my direction. I held my breath. Can he see me? I thought. Can he smell the dead bird at my feet? I watched him. If he roars, I thought in horror, I must not move. I must not move! At last, with a shake of his big shaggy head, he ambled slowly away into the thornbush. For a long time after he left, I remained still, and then I filled the tin with water and ran the long way back to my family.

They were still asleep, but I was afraid to sleep too, for who would guard the partridge from animals? I skinned the bird with my father's knife, then made a fire with acacia twigs. Using a branch as a spit, I held the bird over the flames, not too high and not too low.

When my parents woke, a delicious smell of roasted partridge floated toward them. "Menelik!" my mother cried, her eyes bright with surprise. I told my parents about the lion.

"You were wise not to run," Father said, looking at me in a different way.

Sitting on the ground in the dry wind, we ate the partridge, cutting the juicy breast into tiny pieces for Simcha, putting the food into his mouth, for he seemed too tired to feed himself. While I ate, I thought, I *can* be brave!

As if reading my mind, Father said, "Our Menelik was a brave, strong boy today. He will be brave in Israel too."

At my father's words, I tried to picture myself in Israel, but in my mind all I saw was Israel as it looked on the map above Africa. Tiny and flat, shaped like a knife. "Father," I asked, "are there many like us in Israel?"

"There's been talk of our people being taken to Israel from camps in Sudan," Father answered simply, "but I don't know who takes them, and I don't know how many are taken."

I sipped the stream water for a while, then asked the question that was near my heart. "Do they have teachers in Israel?"

"Yes, Menelik. After we get there, you will go to school."

"But what about my work?"

"You will not work, for you will go to school all day."

All day! It seemed too wonderful to be true. I couldn't even guess the things that take a whole day to teach!

"I want to go to school too," Simcha mumbled with his mouth full. "I want to learn about lions!"

"God-King wish it then," Mother said softly. "When we get to Israel, we will be free." The talk of Israel, the partridge, and the water lifted our spirits when that evening we set out again into the night.

For the next few days we continued very slowly, as Simcha was so weak, we had to carry him most of the time. Though we never saw another partridge, I did use my slingshot to kill eight desert sparrows, and we ate the little fruits growing on the cactus. But we had very little water left.

Early on the fourth evening we saw a tribe of nomads traveling on camels. They were moving toward us in a caravan, and we could not avoid them. In moments we were face to face. Father, who knew many Arabic words from trading in Gondar, boldly asked them, "How far is it to Sudan?"

"Not far," an old man replied, "a day's journey."

"Are you going to Sudan?" one of the men asked, eyeing us closely.

"Yes," my father answered, "we are visiting relatives there."

The men looked at us. Smiles on their lips, disbelief in their eyes.

The old man did not smile, but looked at Simcha, asleep on my father's back. "Give me that tin you're carrying," he commanded me. When I gave it to him, he filled it with milk from a big copper jug at the side of his camel.

"Allah be with you then," the old man said, handing the tin back to me. "Health follow you."

From that day on, we were no longer alone. As we neared the border, we saw masses of people walking toward it. They were Ethiopians, skinny as sticks, trying to escape the famine by crossing into Sudan.

In the distance we could see a guardhouse at the border between Ethiopia and Sudan. On either side Ethiopian and Sudanese soldiers patrolled the border with machine guns. Like angry bees, a noisy crowd of people swarmed at the border. We sat in the scanty shade of an acacia bush while Father walked toward the guardhouse. When at last

he returned, he told us only those with special papers were allowed to cross.

"How will we get into Sudan without special papers?" I asked my parents. But neither one answered me. I looked at the dark sluggish river that ran near the border and the barbed-wire fence beyond. I looked at the soldiers with guns. What will we do if we can't get into Sudan? I thought. Have we come all this way for nothing?

For a whole day we camped at a safe distance from the border. "Aren't we going to go closer?" I asked, and Father answered only, "Not yet."

Mother wanted to ask a guard how to get special papers.

"No!" Father said. "Too risky! If you ask, they'll know you don't have them!"

"Then I will tell them my sister lives in Sudan," Mother declared. "I will say we are visiting her."

"No," Father replied, "they will not believe you."

"Then," Mother suggested frantically, "we must try to enter with a crowd of others — slip in unnoticed with another family."

"No!" Father said. "Too difficult."

"Then we must take the last of our birr and bribe a guard with it."

"Too dangerous," was Father's answer.

"Then how will we get into Sudan?" Mother demanded.

"We will wait and see," Father answered.

"Wait!" Mother exclaimed. "Wait for what? There is nothing here to wait for but death!"

Then Mother aimed words at Father like swift, sharp stones from a slingshot. In return, Father's loud, hard words struck her like blows on an anvil. While my parents quarreled, I sat in the shade and held Simcha on my lap. He did not smile anymore, his eyes were still yellow, and his lips, like mine, were cracked. In the mountains, my mother squeezed the juice from the aloe plant on them, but in this desert no aloe grew. Suddenly I felt anger at my father. He had brought us here with great hope, but no plan. We were very weak now, and far away from our village and our people. My anger grew like fire. Father is a good man, I thought, but he has put us in terrible danger. Now, in a burning desert at a dangerous border, we could go neither forward nor back.

When night fell, we had no meal, for we had no food. Father made us walk far—about four miles up from the guardhouse. There in a deep thicket right before the river, we again made a bed of acacia branches and lay down. But hunger gnawed at me like a dog, and I could not sleep. That is why hours later in the moonlight I saw my father take the iron pliers from his toolbag and slip them into the folds of his shamma. Then I saw him crouch down low, listening to something—like a black panther sensing prey.

The next moment he woke my mother. He whispered to her, then to me. "QUICK! LET'S GO!" My father yanked me up, pulling me onto my feet. "RUN, MENELIK, RUN!"

Following my parents, I ran fast toward the river. My feet sank into the cold, oozing mud. I thought of crocodiles! In silence and darkness we stumbled across the muddy river, our hearts beating in terror.

On the other side ran the barbed-wire fence. With the pliers Father quickly cut the wire, making a big hole. Mother was carrying Simcha, and Father pushed her through. Simcha cried out.

"Shhhh!" Mother hissed fiercely, covering his mouth hard. I climbed after her, then Father went through.

GUNSHOTS!

We ran so fast, I thought my head would burst. There

were thick juniper bushes to our right, and we hid there.
I wanted to say a million things, but we were silent. We
waited and listened. Waited . . . Listened . . . Then we
moved on, walking in the cool dark. Deeper into Sudan.

As we walked, daylight came. Soon other people were
on the roads, and we merged with them, blending in with
the crowds who seemed to be traveling in one direction.

After a while we came to a sign directing us to a refugee camp called Um Raquba. Masses of Ethiopians were
beside us now, walking in that direction. "That is where
you will be given food and shelter," people said. "That is
where we all must go."

It was another two days before we reached the camp.
It was crammed with people! Thousands and thousands.
I had never seen so many people in my life. Many of them
were very sick, their arms and legs even thinner than ours.
A Sudanese man wrote down our names in Arabic, then
took us to a little tent. But the tent was hot and filled with
flies. We were given flour. "Aye!" Mother wailed, for it
too had bugs.

For weeks we lived in the dusty camp. Every day we lined up for rice and water. The water had worms in it, and we had to boil it for a long time. Some days there was milk all the way from America. Many days there was nothing. Some days we ate. Some days we didn't. Once a woman came to put drops in Simcha's eyes, but they did not get better and she never came back.

In Um Raquba we lived in constant fear. Our goal was to get to Israel but not knowing who to trust, we dared not speak of it. We were afraid of what might happen if someone found out we were Beta Israel. We were afraid we might be sent back to Ethiopia. We were afraid someone might blame us for casting an evil spell. But most of all, in our speechless hearts, we were afraid death would touch us too.

Then one morning Mother told us that at the water pump another Beta Israel woman whispered to her, "Have courage. People from Israel will come for us." Mother was too frightened to reply, but the woman continued, "Some Sudanese are helping them. But it is against Sudan law to let us leave for Israel. So do not speak of it. Be patient. Be quiet. Make even your prayers in silence."

We were patient. Day after day, we waited in the camp, surrounded by disease, despair, and death.

One night as we were preparing to sleep, I heard the sly sound of our tent flap slowly opening. In fright I sat up to see a large shadowy figure standing inside our tent. In the sliver of moonlight, I could tell he had the pale skin that is the color of injara. "Are you the people who smell like water?" he asked. "Are you Beta Israel?"

As the man had not called us "Falasha," my father answered honestly, "Yes, we are Beta Israel — how did you know?"

The man did not answer Father's question, but only said, "At three in the morning take your family to the peanut fields. We will take you to Israel, but do not talk of it."

The man's words fell like gold coins on us, yet Father, embarrassed, replied, "I will not know when it is three in the morning."

"Then I'll send someone to wake you," the man answered.

52   The air was still and the night had grown cool when we slipped out of the camp. As we walked to the fields, we saw hundreds of others walking there too, like a great crowd of ghosts in the night. Hundreds of Beta Israel! We wanted to greet each other, to embrace each other, to talk together, to laugh and cry together — but we were told to walk in silence. Complete silence. When we reached the fields, we saw three buses. We are going on buses to Israel! We are going now! Mother squeezed my hand as the light-skinned man read off a list of names. At last he read our names, and just before we climbed the steps of the bus, he pinned the same big number sign on Mother, Father, Simcha, and me. All the Beta Israel crowded onto the buses. We sat on our bundles. We sat in the aisle. We sat on the stairs. We sat on each other. As the bus started its animal groan, I remembered fearfully what the woman had told Mother: "It is against Sudan law to let us leave for Israel."

In the blackness the bus bumped for miles across the fallow fields. But suddenly it stopped, and the doors opened to a deafening sound. "Everyone out!" someone shouted to us in Amharic. Confused and scared, we stumbled over each other to leave the bus, and then we saw it — the enormous white plane that shone in the glow of its own headlights. The plane's engines roared, and there was a smell like gasoline. I had never seen a plane up close, and now it seemed like a terrible beast, but we were being herded quickly toward it. Some people could not go fast, and they were carried on the shoulders of those who could. Up the long stairs we went, into the belly of the plane. There were no seats at all, so the hundreds of us huddled on the floor. Then the door was closed, the roar grew louder, and in seconds we lifted off the ground. My brother was asleep in Father's arms, but I whispered to him anyway, "Simcha, we're flying!"

There were no windows on the plane, and when it dropped lower, people became frightened and prayed like sinners. But at last, with a bang the plane touched the ground, and we rolled to a stop. The doors were opened, and the old and sick carried out. Then we too came out into the bright

dawn. "May God who made the sun to rule by day be glorified," Father murmured fervently as our feet touched the holy land.

"Let the rooster hear the noise of angel wings and crow praise to God!" Mother sang.

All about us Beta Israel cried and prayed. And the Israeli people who watched us come down the stairs called to us, *"Shalom! Barukh Ha-ba!"* Peace to you! Blessed be your coming!

Some Beta Israel were taken right away to hospitals, but we were told to go into one of the red buses waiting by the plane. A Beta Israel man, who wore trousers and a shirt with buttons, came on the bus. He had been in Israel for two years and now told us we were going somewhere near Jerusalem. We were going to what he called an "absorption center." Here families would live for a year, learning Hebrew and new customs. After a year we would leave the absorption center to live wherever we pleased. "Jerusalem . . . Jerusalem . . . Jerusalem. . . ." In awe Mother whispered the holy city's name, making a prayer of the word.

The bus raced along the highway at an incredible

speed, and all we could see was flat land with hills in the distance. Then the bus climbed and curved up these dry steep hills that were golden in the morning light. We rounded a corner and drove into a sort of garden in which stood hundreds of white huts. Mother could not believe it when we were told we would get to live in one of these pretty huts.

That first day we all went to a doctor who gave us soap and strong medicine for Simcha. Then we were given a key to our own home. When we entered the white hut, it was cleaner than anything I had ever seen. And there was magic inside! Whenever we wanted, hot as well as cold water flowed out of a silver pipe. Without even lighting a match, we had fire for cooking. From a small box on the wall, we could make the house warmer. And a big white box that trapped winter inside kept our food snow-cold and fresh.

The next day we all got clean clothes too, with buttons and zippers. Simcha and I got shoes with strings.

But the best thing we got was the food. Three times a day everyone ate together in a big hall. We sat at long tables and ate chicken, beef, lamb, potatoes, eggs, apples,

and oranges—as much as we wanted. We ate a strange bread that had to be cut with a knife. We ate sunset-colored yogurt. And we drank tea made from tiny paper tents dipped in hot water.

"Don't touch your food!" Mother kept reminding Simcha and me, for here the custom was to eat with knives and forks. At first it was so hard that we cheated, using our fingers when no one was looking.

It seemed that in the first month we learned a thousand things. We were all given watches and learned to tell time. When Simcha got better, he learned how to go down a slide, button his shirt, and say the Hebrew names of everything he ate. I learned to write with a pen, and to dial a telephone. Most of all, I learned Hebrew with other boys and girls. Some girls in my class were Beta Israel, but they were older. The boys my age were from Iran and Afghanistan, Syria and Canada. One boy was from Russia, another from the United States.

I wanted to be friends with them, but I was shy. Most of them had been in Israel longer than I, so my Hebrew was less than theirs. When I spoke, my words came out one at a time and often wrong. All my thoughts—all my

ideas were in Amharic. Here, Amharic words were useless as broken tools.

One afternoon I walked to the green field that lay beyond the huts. In the corner of this field was a playground where Simcha was now laughing with other children. From the edge of the field I could look for miles across the Judean hills. I watched an eagle soaring in the sky. Then strangely I remembered the beginning of our journey and the falcon we had seen in the Simen mountains. A wave of homesickness swept over me, and suddenly I longed for the sound of the Sabbath drum, the smell of hot injara, and the closeness of clouds.

"Bo-ooh, Leh-sa-hek!" someone yelled in Hebrew.

"Let's play!"

I turned to see at the opposite end of the field some boys in my class. They had come to play their ball game. One boy they called a "pitcher." He threw a ball, then another boy hit it with a stick and ran around a square as if he were being chased. Watching them for a while, I thought of Josef and our ragball game. I turned to leave, when I heard a sound in the air. A familiar, almost silent sound. Instinctively I turned back to see, from the opposite corner of the field, the ball flying fast in my direction. I ran and with one hand, caught it. One hand. Easy.

Smooth. Cool.

Three of the boys raced over to me, wonder in their eyes.

"Bo! Bo! Leh-sa-hek!"

Come! they called. Come play!

I threw the ball back to the pitcher. Then I ran to join the game.

For thousands of years Jews have lived in the high mountains of Ethiopia. Once rulers of a flourishing African kingdom that numbered more than half a million, disease, famines, and wars reduced their population to less than 28,000 by 1980. Living in remote villages scattered on the high tabletop mountains in the Gondar province, the Beta Israel had become an impoverished, oppressed community, feared and shunned by their Muslim and Christian neighbors. Despite their oppression, these Jews, who called themselves Beta Israel, clung to their 2,000-year-old heritage, holding a stubborn belief in the biblical prophecy that one day they would return to Israel.

The overthrow of Ethiopia's emperor Haile Selassie in the 1970's by the military set into motion years of turmoil and tyranny. The Marxist military government that came to power in 1978 was especially harsh on the Beta Israel who longed to live in Israel, a nation branded by the government as "Zionist imperialist." Any attempt to leave Ethiopia was seen as an affront to the government and punished by torture or death.

By 1984 Ethiopia descended into chaos, and it was at this time that drought caused a famine which swept through the country like a plague. In a desperate quest for food, thousands of Ethiopians trekked to Sudan where international refugee camps had been set up. In this period thousands of Beta Israel made their way out of Ethiopia.

The mysterious, concealed rescue of the Ethiopian Jews from the camps of Sudan was the combined effort of Israeli secret agents, American and European volunteers, and certain Sudanese officials. Beginning in November 1984, nearly 10,000 Beta Israel refugees were evacuated in a number of nighttime airlifts named "Operation Moses." In 1986 news of the secret mission leaked out, and several of those who helped the Ethiopian Jews escape to Israel were imprisoned or killed. All entry into Sudan was stopped, and the remaining Jews in Ethiopia were more persecuted than ever.

Then, in 1991 the Israeli government pulled off another miraculous mission, "Operation Solomon," which rescued 14,000 Beta Israel from Ethiopia in a 36-hour secret airlift.

Today the life of the Beta Israel in the high mountains of Gondar is ended, and a new, free, yet very different life in Israel has begun.

J
S

Schur, Maxine.

When I left my
village.

$14.99

DATE			
MAY 9 1996			
JUN 17 1996			
APR 21 1997			
SEP 04 1997			
NOV 12 1997			

BAKER & TAYLOR